Rookie reader

Fast-Draw Freddie

By Bobbie Hamsa
Illustrated by Susan Miller

SCHOLASTIC INC.
New York Toronto London Auckland Sydney
Mexico City New Delhi Hong Kong Buenos Aires

To Viktor
—S. M.

Reading Consultants
Linda Cornwell
Coordinator of School Quality and Professional Improvement
(Indiana State Teachers Association)

Katharine A. Kane
Education Consultant
(Retired, San Diego County Office of Education
and San Diego State University)

ISBN 0-516-24122-2

Published by Scholastic Inc., 555 Broadway, New York, NY 10012.

12 11 10 9 8 7 6 5 4 3 2 1 2 3 4 5 6 7/0

Printed in the U.S.A. 10

First Scholastic printing, January 2002

Fast-Draw Freddie
draws pictures fast.

Big pictures.

Small pictures.

Short pictures.

Tall pictures.

Thin pictures.

Fat pictures.

Mouse pictures.

Cat pictures.

Pictures of Mom.

Pictures of Dad.

Pictures of Grandma
that aren't too bad.

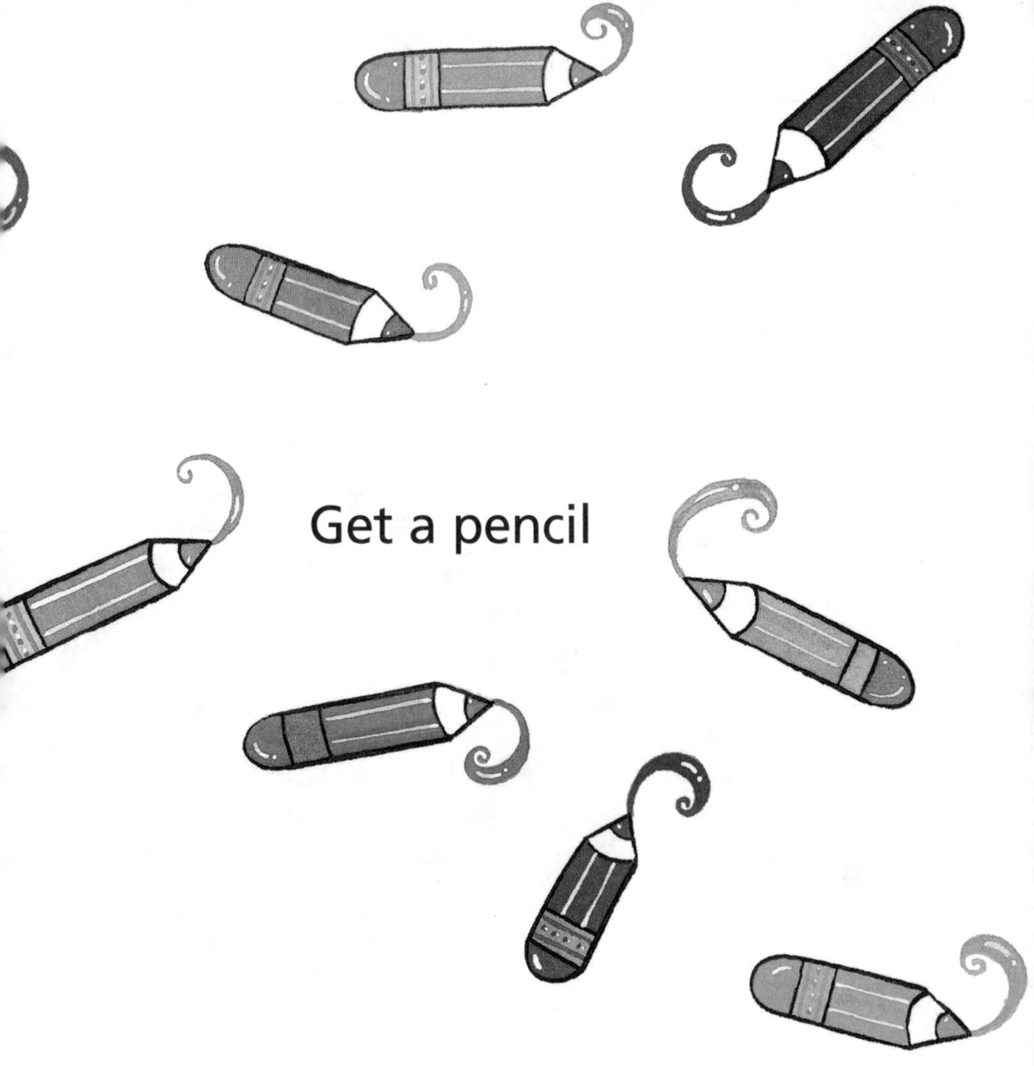

Get a pencil

and a paper or two.

You can be a Fast Draw, too!

Word List (31 words)

a
and
aren't
bad
be
big
can
cat
Dad
draw
draws
fast
fat
Freddie
get
Grandma
Mom
mouse
of
or
paper
pencil
pictures
short
small
tall
that
thin
too
two
you

About the Author

Bobbie Hamsa was born and raised in Nebraska and has a Bachelor of Arts Degree in English Literature. She is an advertising copywriter, writing print, radio, and television copy for many accounts. She is also the author of many children's books. Bobbie lives in Omaha with her husband, Dick Sullivan, and children, John, Tracy, and Kenton.

About the Illustrator

Susan Miller has illustrated many picture books. *Fast-Draw Freddie* is her fifth book in the Rookie Reader series. She loves drawing fast in her studio in Terryville, Connecticut, where she lives with her husband, two children, one cat, one dog, and a very fast kitten.